The Tale of Steven

BY REBECCA SUGAR, CREATOR OF STEVEN UNIVERSE
ILLUSTRATED BY ELLE MICHALKA AND ANGIE WANG

ABRAMS, NEW YORK

THIS BOOK
BELONGS TO

Read it like THIS!

What are you doing? You're holding the book upside-down!

She was impossible to understand, impossible to ignore, and impossible to control.

Pink was as silly as she was small.

nce upon a time, there
were four Diamonds.
White, Yellow, Blue, and
the littlest Diamond, Pink.

But Blue and Yellow spoiled her with treasures, listened to her nonsense, and enabled her terrible behavior.

W

hite knew
better than
to indulge
Pink's whims.

It was up to White to keep Pink in her place.

Only White was immune to Pink's ridiculous influence.

O

ne day, Pink,
difficult as ever,
ran off to another
planet.

S he foolishly thought she could escape her Diamond role by disguising herself as a lowly Rose Quartz.

S he belonged on a beautiful planet, amongst strange and whimsical creatures who treated her well.

S he stubbornly stayed on that Gem-forsaken world—

H iding from the Diamonds, hiding from her Homeworld—

Fine! See how you fare without me!

And ultimately hiding from herself, inside an unwitting creature.

To have a beautiful half-human child.

He was always hearing about her, and she sounded so amazing.

He knew she wanted to become human, and she wanted to become him, and that as long as Steven had her Gem they couldn't both exist.

The more he learned about her, the more it started to scare him—

OF COURSE there's one right way. Now hold the book correctly.

And would never find a way back to her horrendous old home....

I guess there are several stories from different angles.

Maybe there isn't one right way to hold the book.

It was only a matter of time before Pink came crawling back.

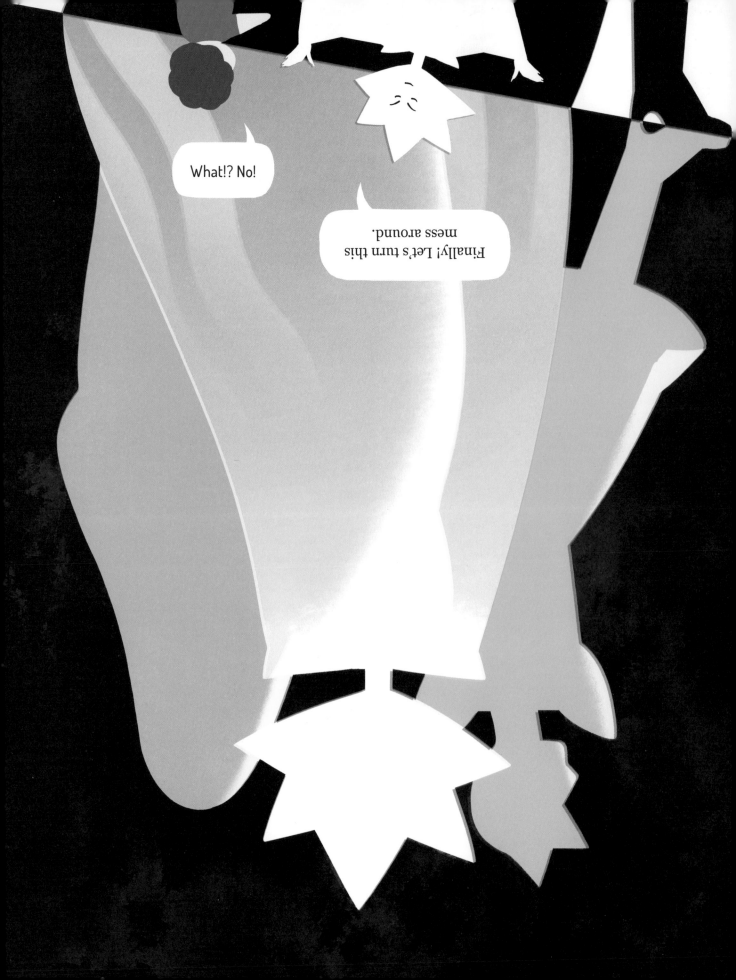

a nd never be
picked apart
by the other
Diamonds.

D esperate
for White to
correct her.

T hough he couldn't
be sure, he had to
believe—

Believe he wasn't her, believe in himself, and—

She hoped her child would somehow, someday understand what a difference it makes to tell your own story, and—

White knew Pink would never change, and no one on this or any other world would prove her wrong, but—

Once upon a time

Once
upon
a time

Once
upon
a time

THIS BOOK BELONGS TO

Steven Universe ☆